LYNN MONTGOMERY

BUTT UGLY

iLLustrAted by

Terrie Redding

A ZuZu Petals Book

Santa Barbara * Dallas

ZuZu Petals Publishing
2311 Garden Street
Santa Barbara, CA 93105

Book Design by Richard Kriegler

The text of this book is set in Mrs. Eaves.
The illustrations are pen and ink drawings with computer coloration.

Printed by Pinnacle Press in the United States of America
on post-consumer waste, recycled paper, processed chlorine free,
using vegetable based inks and renewable energy. (YEAAAA Earth!)

10 9 8 7 6 5 4 3 2

Library of Congress Control Number: 2008928910
Montgomery, Lynn.
Butt Ugly/written by Lynn Montgomery, illustrated by Terrie Redding.

Summary: A proud, fearless dog remembers his miserable life when he
was a scrawny, greenish runt, hiding in the corner and saddled with the
label, Butt Ugly.

ISBN 978-0-9815724-0-6

VISIT US ON THE WORLD WIDE WEB
www.zuzupetalsbooks.com

NEW LEAF PAPER®
ENVIRONMENTAL BENEFITS STATEMENT
of using post-consumer waste fiber vs. virgin fiber

ZuZu Petals saved the following resources by using New Leaf Primavera Gloss, made with 80% recycled
fiber and 60% post-consumer waste, elemental chlorine free, and manufactured with electricity that is
offset with Green-e® certified renewable energy certificates.

trees	water	energy	solid waste	greenhouse gases
17 fully grown	7,765 gallons	11 million Btu	835 pounds	1,854 pounds

Calculations based on research by Environmental Defense Fund and other members of the Paper Task Force.

www.newleafpaper.com

To Hannah and Austin

To Ana and John Patrick

To Sparky (RIP), the original Butt Ugly who showed up on our doorstep one day and found a boy to love him.

… and to a world where every child and every mutt is a "first pick."

A portion of the profits of this book will go to support CALM (Child Abuse Listening and Mediation) and animal rescue organizations.

BUTT UGLY

Hey kids, I'm going to tell you a story. You see, I wasn't always such a handsome dog. No siree. When I was born, everyone screamed –

That pup is messed up! All snaggle-toothed and wrinkly, with three little hairs sticking up from his butt. That pup is BUTT UGLY!

And that's what they called me - **BUTT UGLY.**
Hard enough being a greenish runt in a litter of
thirteen walloping tail-waggers.

Way worse when you're saddled with a name like -

BUTT UGLY.

Made me feel puny, inside and out.

And as I got punier, the other tail-waggers got perkier. Fang needed someone to snarl at. Princess needed someone to prance at. And they all needed someone to laugh at.

HA HA!! BUTT UGLY!

I crawled under the blanket so they wouldn't have to see me and I wouldn't have to hear them.

And that was my life, until one morning, the two-legged owner put an ad in the paper:

Adorable puppies for Sale

I hung my head and slouched to the corner.

My brothers and sisters wiggled and waggled about who was the cutest, cuddliest puppy.

And who would be picked first.

Princess decided to show off for the families.
She ordered a pile-on-puppy-pyramid.

Guess who was smooshed, flat-face on the bottom?

Yours truly, BUTT UGLY.

One by one, the puppies found new homes.

But no one wanted BUTT UGLY.

Maybe that was good, I told myself between sniffles.
Maybe I could stay with Momma in the cozy house
where I was born. Momma thought it was a grand
tooting idea.

Momma never called me BUTT UGLY.

Momma thought all her pups were first-picks.

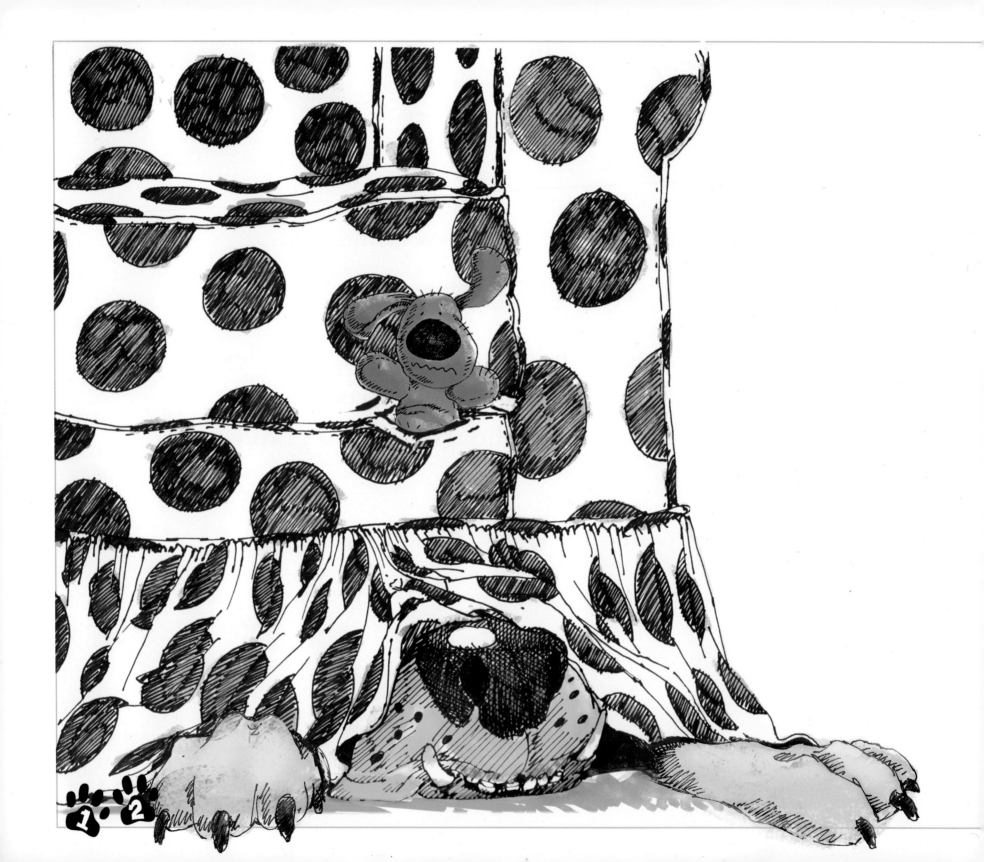

But I heard the owner talking about me and she had other plans.

BIG PLANS.   SCARY PLANS.

THREE HAIRS STICKING STRAIGHT UP

ON YOUR HAIRY BUTT PLANS!

I back-scooted and scrunched under the couch.

She dragged me back out.

HELP! HELP!

My puppy heart pounded. She slapped a collar
around my neck and sprayed something sneezy
on my three little hairs.

Then she smooshed me into a basket,
smothered me with a scratchy blanket and
smashed heavy boxes on me.

HELP!

She raced down the street. I sneaked a peek.

HELP! HELP!!

Finally we stopped. She plopped me down.

I heard a ringing. A pounding. Then she ran away and just <u>left me there?!?</u>

Oh Man. Oh Man. I can't believe it...

Im a ding-dong ditch!!!

I felt the cold creep through the basket. And just when I was ready to make a run for it - I heard the door open...

"Hello?" A small voice called.

I felt a sneeze coming, but I trapped it inside.

"Hey Mom, someone left me a present!"

Nice trick soften him up with cookies so he doesn't scream when he finds me hidden in the-

AACHOOOOOOO!

Oh no...

Oh no.....

His pokey fingers grabbed me and held me high in the air,
dangling like a doofus.

A BUTT UGLY DOOFUS!

The boy just stared and stared...

"Mom…"

It wasn't a scream, not yet.

"Mom… he's…"

Go on and say it. I can take it. Nothing I ain't heard before…

"He's mine! Right? What's your name, little fellow?"

He reached for my collar. I plastered on my best snaggle-toothed grin. But I knew, as soon as he read my name he wouldn't want me. What kid wants a dog named…

"Fred. He looks like a Fred, doesn't he, Mom?"

"It's a perfect name. Happy Birthday, honey. I asked them to save the pick of the litter for you."

"Thanks, Mom!"

Then that boy gave me a squeeze and a wet smoocher on the snout. I smooched him right back.

"I love you, Fred!" said that marvelous boy.

And the more he called me **Fred,** the less puny I grew, inside and out. Until magically, I transformed from -

BUTT UGLY PUP...

To
Fabulous, Fearless Fred

LONG LIVE THE
FRED!

THE END